ISBN: 978-0-615-65279-5

Printed in the U.S.A by Bookmasters
30 Amberwood Pkwy, Ashland, OH 44805
M9838 8/2012

TravlinBug'z Books
PO Box 2350
Attleboro, MA 02703-2350

D0543938

To The Guardians
The Journey Begin'z

Thank you to Mom and Dad
My first fan'z, I love you both

To the real "Deanna"
I love you Boo Boo!!

To the real "Sam"
"THAT'S FUNNY"

THE TALE OF THE
TravlinBug'z

A Continuing Adventure
The Journey Begin'z

by Jason Graham
TravlinBug'z Books

The Tale of the TravlinBug'z

A Continuing Adventure
The Journey Begin'z

CHAPTER ONE
Good to be home, but for how long

CHAPTER TWO
Let's get started, the construction begin'z

CHAPTER THREE
First flight, working out The Bug'z

CHAPTER FOUR
Many miles away

CHAPTER FIVE
One loose nut, might be a problem

CHAPTER SIX
VICTOR SPOIL'Z

CHAPTER SEVEN
The masterpiece is born

CHAPTER EIGHT
At long last the "KEY"

CHAPTER NINE
Tightening up loose ends

CHAPTER TEN
Deanna Driftwood BUG'Z N' HUG'Z

CHAPTER ELEVEN
The Guardian's Club, our secret is safe

CHAPTER TWELVE
Sophie's surprise

CHAPTER THIRTEEN
Where to next, the adventure continues

CHAPTER ONE

Good to be home,
but for how long

"My wings are tired"

Sam could feel the cool, salty mist blow on his face as he held on tight to Travis' pack and Taylor's pouch. Even Sam, with his amazing strength, had begun to get tired. After days of flying, the Bug'z started to realize how long they had been trapped in Claude's trunk on the ship. "My wings are tired. We have been flying for days. I have to rest soon, I don't think it could be WORSER," said Sam. "Sam, U rest, U rust!!" said Travis. "We need to reach the Island. Sam, just a while longer. I calculated the distance from the stars, it's only a little bit further, you can do it Sam, hang in there," said Taylor. "Me… you are the ones hanging in there not me.

I'm just getting a bit tired that's all, what are you two carrying anyway?" said Sam. Finally off in the distance a strange rock formation arose from the mist. Suddenly Sam could see "That Place" the one he had become so fond of where he and Father had met. "I was right, my calculations were correct and I must say we made good time," said Taylor. Sam couldn't tell how long he had been flying, he was just happy to be home but for how long... The landing was, well not as soft as it could have been, but no one ever... complained. Travis looked at Sam and said, "You always come through in a pinch. My friend, get some rest, you deserve it but not that much, you know what happens." Travis smiled at Sam with that Thank-You look. It was good to be home but the feeling didn't last long. "You know we cannot stay long when Claude finds out we have escaped, he will surely try to get back to the Island. We can't be here when they arrive, we must warn all the others that our secret is out. We have quite a few friends and family we are going to need to find and warn. There is much for us to do," said Taylor in her concerned voice. "Right now I am much too tired for... "TRAVLIN," said Sam. "You rest Sam, you will need your strength, I have an idea. Travis come with me, we have been hanging around too long already," said Taylor.

Travis smiled at Taylor as she didn't make jokes too often and he knew she had a plan. Taylor opened her pouch and pulled out an old journal, one of her favorite sketch books lay inside. From inside she pulled out plans for what looked like a log with wings. "It's a flying machine and it will work." Taylor smiled. Travis and Sam looked at one another and at the same time said, "How long have you been holding on to this great invention?" What else do you have in that pouch?" said Travis. Taylor just smiled, "Oh awhile, but there was never a need before. I know it will work. I calculated everything and the best part is everything we need is right here."

She pointed to their Huts. "We can recycle all we need and it will save us lots of time, and time I know all about. We will be able to travel great distances in a short amount of time. Sam, we will need your wings to power the machine so rest up, you deserve it. Travis and I can begin, Thank you Sam," said Taylor as she pecked Sam on the cheek and he turned from green to red.

END OF CHAPTER ONE

CHAPTER TWO

Let's get started, the construction begin'z

"Are you sure this will fly?"

There was quite abuzzz as they made their way over to the Huts. "This is amazing Taylor, most of what we need is right here almost like you planned it," said Travis. Taylor just smiled. Taylor knew her role on the Island but many times dreamed of "TRAVLIN" like the others. In a way this was her chance to prove to herself there was more to her than her books and journals. She was ready for this adventure. "I know you are tired Sam but shortly you will need your strength," said Taylor. Travis began to go through his backpack which had almost everything you could imagine stuffed inside. Way down deep in a small jar was a brass tack. "Taylor, may I see those plans?" Travis asked politely still amazed. Taylor tore out the pages from the sketch book and handed them over to Travis. Travis took the pages, studied them for a moment and shook his head, then tacked them onto a tree. He looked back at Taylor and said, "What are you waiting for, U rest, U rust." They both began to work steadily as Sam rested a while on his hammock. After a short nap Sam arose much like he always did, ready to go. The others had already begun to lay out the frame-work for the flying machine. Sam got right into it and studied the plans. Piece by piece the Huts came apart, sad at first, but they all knew it had to be done. The three Bug'z worked long into the night until it was time to rest and take a much needed break. Neither Sam, Travis nor Taylor ever spoke of what happened on the ship, they all knew what needed to be done and stayed steady on their task working as a team. "We will get back at it when the night ends," said Travis. "We are making good time," said Taylor. "I am feeling much better already," said Sam. As he looked at the plans on the tree he asked, "What is this piece here?" Taylor smiled. "You will see in the light, get some rest Sam."

After some much needed rest, the Bug'z returned to work on the flying machine. The plans were very detailed for a sketch and all the pieces seemed to fit together. There was no arguing from the boys, they knew what Taylor had designed was exactly what they needed. There were plenty of wood timbers between the three Huts, and the best part-cleanup would be easy, almost everything was used up, nothing was left behind right down to the last nail that Sam hung his hat on...

"Are you sure this will fly?" said Travis with a smile, as all three stood back looking at Taylor's masterpiece. "Sam you must go over everything to make sure it's tight with your strength, it's going to be a long flight, we don't need anything coming loose... "said Taylor. Sam smiled, then began working. With his heart aching, he looked at his hammock stretched out and twisted into some piece he didn't understand. "Well, IT COULD BE WORSER, or not." Taylor and Travis began to put together all the supplies they would need for the journeys ahead. "We have to travel light," said Travis. Taylor then asked, "Who's first?" Travis answered, "That's easy,

17

we must start with DEANNA
DRIFTWOOD the youngest of us all,
and my little cousin. At this time
of year, I have a good feeling. I know
where we can find her," said Travis.

END OF CHAPTER TWO

CHAPTER THREE

First flight,
working out The Bug'z

So the journey begin'z

"I can calculate the shortest distance we need to go to get to Deanna. Are you sure she will be where you say she is?" said Taylor. "She will be no other place, trust me!!" said Travis. Sam turned back from the machine and met his friends. "Well I'm sure going to miss this place, I'm not sure I'm ready for another adventure so soon but IT COULD BE WORSER," he said with his crooked smile. "We are all going to miss the Island. There is no time now, we have to get moving, right Travis?" said Taylor. Travis looked at them both and said, "You know what I have to say!! So I won't even say it. It's not the last time we are going to be here together on this Island, it's special

21

and our home. It will be here when we return, but for now we have a mission to accomplish and lots of friends we have to warn. We had better get going or IT COULD BE WORSER," said Travis, as Sam looked at him funny. The three Bug'z took one last look around making sure not to leave any trace that they had been there, just in case the others were able to find their way back. After loading up everything they needed, Taylor said to Sam, "Well it's your turn Sam." Sam looked at the special harness she and Travis had configured. "Are you sure this will work?" said Sam. "If my calculations are correct, you will never get tired again.

I took into consideration, the size of
your wings and what force it will take
to drive the machine. All together
the wind velocity and other calculations
we need to stay in the air have been
taken into consideration, it will work!!"
she said with a smile. "OK I guess I
don't even have to say it," said Sam.
"Let's give it a whirl." Sam began to
flap his wings and all of the rigging
and pullies and ropes began to transfer
Sam's wing speed and force into the
larger wings of the machine. "It's
working!! It's... working!!" said Sam.
Sam began to move his wings as if
he was flying. "This isn't as bad as I
thought," said Sam. The machine
began to shake and move. Suddenly

it began to bounce around and lift off of the ground. "A little bit faster Sam!!" said Travis, "U rest, U rust." The faster Sam moved his wings, the higher the machine began to move into the air. "You're doing it Sam, it's working!!" said Taylor, almost surprised. "If everything works as I planned and my calculations are correct and we consider the head wind and our speed, I can figure out how long the journey should take to get to Deanna. Let's just say the first flight we are going to have to work the Bug'z out," said Taylor. Sam and Travis looked at each other and smiled, and then Sam asked "WHAT BUG'Z?" They all laughed for the first time in a long time. As the machine lifted off into the air, the Bug'z looked back at the Island for what they hoped would not be the last time...

Up through the clouds they rose to the warm, sunny blue skies. "This is working better than I had expected. Luckily the weather is on our side, for now anyways. Looks like clear sailing," said Taylor. "Sailing?" said Sam, "I thought we were flying the whole way, I'm done with ships!!" The machine began to move forward slowly at first making popping and squealing sounds. "Sam faster, faster!!" said Travis. The faster Sam flapped his wings, the faster the machine began to move. "Who is steering this thing anyways?" said Sam. He noticed no real controls anywhere in sight. "Well no one," said Taylor in her what do you mean voice. "What do you mean no one?" said Sam looking more puzzled than usual. Taylor began to let him in on her secret. "Well Sam, do you remember the night on the ship when the "little one" let us go free? Before we flew off dodging the lanterns, I took a quick peek through Victor'z key hole in his cabin door. It was this, Sam." Taylor pulled out a small wooden and metal box. "I... memorized the design and recreated it exactly as he had made his." "But what does it do?" Sam asked puzzled. "Travis, your compass please," said Taylor. As Travis handed over his trusty compass he too was puzzled. Taylor strapped the compass into the first hole on the strange little box she had mounted on the front of the flying machine in a special holder she had designed. Then she pulled out her trusty pocket watch and snapped it securely into its place in the second hole. Finally she was happy with the placement with her and Travis' most special belongings.

She then asked Sam for one of his many blank tickets he carried around, hoping someday there would be a destination on one of them for him to travel to. "Today Sam, is your lucky day," said Taylor. Taylor thanked Sam and gently fed one of his tickets into the small slot in the front of the device. Suddenly Travis' compass began to spin out of control and the watch hands on Taylor's pocket watch began to spin backwards- out of character for such a perfect piece of machinery. It began to vibrate and buzz and make horrible noises. Suddenly out of the other end came a colorful postcard with a picture of Deanna Driftwood on it with no words just the latitude of

28

N 43° 50'15.48" and longitude of
W 70° 32'00.35"- the perfect whereabouts of Travis' little cousin. "What's
it say?" said Sam. "Well Travis is
right, if I read these correctly,
Deanna is right where we thought she
would be." So the journey begins.
"But how?" said Sam. "You see that
Victor is a pretty intelligent guy, but
little does he know, so are We," said
Taylor. Then they all smiled. Long
into the journey after many starry
nights and warm summer breezes,
Sam spoke, "IT COULD BE WORSER...
you know, this harness is not as
cramped as those jars were. This is a
much better view too than the inside
of that old trunk. If it wasn't for the

"little one" who knows where we would be now. I miss the "little one". Travis and Taylor agreed all of her kind should be like her. As the journey grew longer, the ideas of who should be warned next, after Deanna, buzzed about the machine. There are so many, we must come up with a plan to tell all the rest. "How do we do that?" said Sam. Taylor spoke up, "I've been thinking about it for awhile now and once we land I think we will have another piece of the puzzle." "I didn't know you brought a puzzle," said Sam. Travis rolled his eyes under his glasses. "Keep your wings moving Sam, U rest, U rust." In a softer voice he said, "Sam, you are doing a great job and if I haven't told you both yet, Thank-You." The machine was quiet, Taylor broke the silence. "How long has it been anyway since you have seen Deanna?" Travis thought about it for a moment and his eyes rolled back and forth under his glasses almost as if he was remembering the exact date and time. "I can't really say," said Travis. "It's been far too long, in any case. But I think of her from time to time. She is like the rest of us, loves Travlin about the world. I thought those days were long behind me, but we have a new reason now, not only to take care of the Island, but to take care of all the Bug'z so they don't find themselves in the same predicament as we did trapped in a jar at the bottom of a trunk," said Travis. "We are doing just fine," said Taylor. "At this rate, it's not long now and we should all make it in one piece, right Sam?" "One piece, well I've always been one piece!!" said Sam. As they began "TRAVLIN" closer to their destination, the Bug'z could feel something, but not one of the three said it out loud. They all looked at one another and could almost tell what the other was thinking.

END OF CHAPTER THREE

CHAPTER FOUR

Many miles away

Whale Rock...

Many miles away on her own Island was Deanna Driftwood enjoying her day in the water just like every other day. Her painted toes all scuffed up from playing on the beach in her favorite blue sandals. Being the youngest of the Bug'z, Deanna was very energetic and playful. She just loved the water. She could spend all day just being in or around any lake, stream or ocean. This is where she felt the most comfortable. She loved many places she had traveled to in the world but at this time of year this was the only spot for her. The temperature was just right and the sunsets were like no other place on earth. She had come to the Island by chance and if she had it her way, she would never leave. The dirt roads and blueberries made her feel right at home. The Island was full of ripe, big berries this time of year and what makes a better snack than that? Right off the bush she would pick them after a hard day of playing in the water. Always by her side was her trusty IPod with all the music she loved. The only time she took it off was in the water and most of the time, not even then. It all depended on what sport she was doing at the time. Her pink life vest was her other trusty companion. Always on, "Safety First!!" she would always say, especially when in the big waves after a storm or tubing. She had become quite fond of one beach in particular on the back side of the Island where the sand was perfect for sandcastles... and what sandcastles she would build!! Up early every morning with a smile, she would put on her sunblock and get right into the day's activities. At least once a day she would swim out to her favorite spot out on the lake. She would climb out on a special rock, a special place that reminded her of home. It resembled a whale coming out of the water and the nickname that was given to it was "WHALE ROCK." Boy it was fun to jump off this rock and to this day I bet she can't even count as high as the amount of times she jumped off that rock.

If you asked her she would probably say, "a couple times I guess." As Deanna went about her daily routine, little did she know, her older cousin Travis and friends were on their way.

END OF CHAPTER FOUR

CHAPTER FIVE

One loose nut,
might be a problem

"We might have a problem."

"This isn't as easy as I thought," said Sam. "Oh you're doing just fine," said Travis. "Anyway we are making great time," said Taylor. "The machine seems to be holding together quite nicely, there are a few things I would change in my design, but like anything else, it's a work in progress." Just then, Sam looked over the side of the machine. He noticed one nut he had forgotten to tighten before they lifted off from the Island. It seemed to be spinning loose, even worser, he had forgotten to put the cotter pin in and bend it over. This wasn't just any nut, it was the main nut that held the wings to the pulley system that Sam was harnessed into. He had meant to, but the wrench was too small and the cotter pin was too large. When he went to get a smaller one on the Island, Travis had pulled him aside for help on loading one of the heavy supplies on the machine, Sam had forgotten to get back to it... this could get WORSER he thought to himself. "Ah Travis, Taylor, we might have a problem!!"

END OF CHAPTER FIVE

CHAPTER SIX

VICTOR SPOIL'Z

44

Little did the Bug'z know, this was not their only problem, you see the Bug'z had no idea of what had happened since their escape from the ship-what had happened to the "little one" and the others. Nothing was known about Claude's demise and what had happened on that, what was supposed to be, his "Greatest Night" ever. So much had happened to everyone who had been on that voyage, but the one who had changed the most was Victor Spoil'z. Once a quiet, handsome young... machinist, Victor had become obsessed with finding the Island and returning the Bug'z to Claude. For you see after that fateful night in the alleyway, Victor could no longer control his thoughts. They would rush into his head as if someone had turned on a faucet. He spent hours filling notebooks with sketches and designs of extraordinary mechanical marvels. Some to this day, the world has yet to see. Victor had become somewhat of a recluse... accompanied only by his passion. He had lost touch with almost everyone who had meant anything to him. Almost everyone!! In an old abandoned warehouse that had been left to him near the shipyard, he had begun to assemble his masterpiece with one plan in mind. Find and capture THE TRAVLINBUG'Z. Not just Sam, Travis and Taylor, but all of them he had heard about on the

Island. Day and night Victor worked and used every last penny to create a mechanical marvel that piece by piece, when assembled, would create a devise he so needed to track the Bug'z. At the center of it all, was the one piece that he had crafted so long ago, the now infamous magnifying glass. Victor'z warehouse was not much to look at from outside, but if you were lucky enough to step through the doors into the dimly lit hallways, you would see at the end, a large open loft with machines lined up in perfect order.

In the early morning as the sun rose, the beams of sun rays would shine through the large windows at the top of the building as vast as it was. This was the time of day Victor would use the light to his advantage. Twisting and shaping metal, turning pieces on the lathe all done with precision accuracy, all with one thing in mind. If he took the time now, it would pay off one day. In his mind he knew, that day would come. Once again there would be a... "GREATEST NIGHT"

END OF CHAPTER SIX

CHAPTER SEVEN

The masterpiece
is born

Day and night Victor worked.

Victor, the man, who was once so routine had begun to think more freely. He would experiment with different metals and even create his own formulas, there was nothing he could not create. He toiled untold hours to create his "masterpiece" with only one drawback, when it was completed - its sheer size. The warehouse was almost completely filled to the ceiling, no longer were sun rays able to find their way in. Only lanterns dimly lit the enormous area. This never stopped Victor as he stood and stared at the machine through his goggles, arms crossed, always thinking. Then he... began, twisting and turning, testing every bolt, fuse, connection and if it wasn't good enough, he would make it again, better than the first. Refining each piece making it smaller and smaller, creating a new quest for himself. To become complete he would need to somehow stay in touch with the machine. As he stretched to reach for a rod to weld with, he looked at his father's old worn welding leathers that he had fashioned to protect his arms, when in a stroke of genius he took them off and threw them onto his work bench, that only had a small area left. They could support a machine manageable enough that could be strapped to his body and could be linked, somehow, to his masterpiece. Hour after hour he spent trimming and fitting, shaping again, all of the pieces he would need. A coil for heat, a fan to cool, supports were machined and held in place always leaving room for expansion. Carefully, piece after piece was fitted to perfection. Once assembled this engineering feat may have even surpassed the machine as his greatest triumph. In a moment of happiness, only a moment, he turned to the machine. With a red hot branding iron he had fashioned, on the front pocket which held all his tools, he burned into the old soft leather, his initials VS. This was the first time Victor had ever put his name on any of his creations. Victor worked long into the next day documenting every piece. Another device would be built right away he thought to himself, then hidden only in a spot where Victor knew of its whereabouts. Or so he thought...

END OF CHAPTER SEVEN

CHAPTER EIGHT

At long last the "KEY"

THE MASTERPIECE

56

At long last after an untold amount of time Victor was ready. On a cold, rainy morning, after many tests and retests it finally came to throwing the last switch. This would be his finest moment, for now. Without hesitation, with all the calculations taken and considered, he pulled down on the large knife blade switch. The crackling of electricity could be heard through-out the entire building, but yet, there was no one there to see it come alive. The machine was born at that moment, at the same time, a small piece of Victor changed forever. As he walked from the breaker panel over to the center of the machine, he lifted off his goggles and stared directly into the center piece - the magnifying glass. He waited for what seemed to be forever until blurry images appeared, but he could only hear voices and buzzing sounds. The same buzzing sounds he heard as he forced Sam into the jar that night on the Island, following the orders of Claude Philippe. At first he thought he failed, all this work was for nothing. But then he realized, the glass he had created not to harm the Bug'z was still doing the job it was created for. Attempt after attempt was made to create a new glass insert for the magnifying glass. So close!! In all the building of the machine, he could not remember the formula. He had placed it in one of his many journals, there was a library full. Which one held the answer? Victor finally devised a formula he thought would work, but in his haste forgot one key element. The mold was created and a new glass was blown into shape and once completed, placed into the old handle. He placed it back into the holder that he had machined. A perfect fit!! Success!! Now the time had come, he had all the pieces in place. He now held the key to track "THE TRAVLINBUG'Z!!"

END OF CHAPTER EIGHT

CHAPTER NINE

Tightening up loose ends

"IT COULD BE WORSER!!"

Sam watched the nut vibrate with both eyes, big and small. Every time he flapped his wings, the machine's wings would vibrate and loosen the nut more and more. "Ah, Travis, Taylor we might have a problem," said Sam - softly at first, as the others were discussing their location. "Travis, I think you need to see this," said Sam. Taylor and Travis looked at each other. "What is it Sam?" said Taylor. "Are you getting tired? It's not far now, by my... calculations, it's right over those trees on the horizon," Sam answered, quite calmly. "Well, I think I should tell you something, you both know my biggest fear." "Well, sure" they both answered, "forgetting what you forgot about, right?" Suddenly, Travis knew the problem. Travis climbed over Taylor to Sam. Looked him right in the eyes, big and little then said softly, not to alarm Taylor. "What nut or cotter pin am I looking for Sam?" Sam moved his eyes down to the nut under the wings coming loose. "Really Sam!!" said Travis. "The big one under the wings that holds it all together?" Travis winked at Sam and said, "Well IT COULD BE WORSER, at least its only one? Right?" Travis climbed back over Taylor, who at this point knew something was the matter. The boys were protecting her, as they always did. Travis reached into his backpack and pulled out a spare cotter pin.

Taylor then said, "I thought that I had calculated the right amount for the job. Did I make a miscalculation Travis?" "No time, Taylor, U rest, U rust." As he climbed back over her, hooking his backpack onto the top of the bolt, Travis then hung over the side of the flying machine, moving very quickly as fast as he could, he put the pin into the hole and spread it open so that the nut could not run all the way off the threads. Then he hand tightened the nut back as tight as he could, all while hanging high above the water. "That should do it Sam," said Travis, "You were right." Sam just smiled eyes wide, looking at Travis with his thank you face.

"What was that all about?" said Taylor, as Travis climbed back over her into his seat. "Nothing really, Sam thought he heard a noise. It was nothing. I can see we can take a closer look when we land, to make sure everything is still tight, right Sam?" said Travis. "Right!!" said Sam. "Tight, got it." Travis never spoke of it again, and that's what friends do. Travis knew he could count on Sam for almost... anything. This time it was Travis' turn to come through in a pinch. In all the excitement, the Bug'z hadn't realized the strange little box that held Travis' compass and Taylor's watch began to buzz and make horrible noises again. "This is it!!" said Taylor.

"Sam let's slow it down a bit and bring it in slowly." Sam was happy to do anything at this point to know that they were landing and he would finally get some rest. Well, after he got a chance to tighten up a few loose ends...

END OF CHAPTER NINE

CHAPTER TEN

Deanna Driftwood
BUG'Z N' HUG'Z

"Why are you really here?"

Deanna Driftwood had been going about her normal routine. While jumping off "WHALE ROCK" she noticed off in the distance what looked like a giant bird coming out of the sky. The only thing about this bird, it didn't look like it had been flying too long. I hope it's not hurt she thought to herself, it looked awful unstable as if it might fall out of the sky. Deanna just stood watching, hoping it was ok. Suddenly as it began to get closer, she realized this was no bird, but some flying machine. Right then a strange feeling came over her, something she hadn't felt in a long time. Not since she had left the Island. Travis stood up and began waving in excitement.

Taylor and Sam hadn't seen him like this "ever". The flying machine began to turn and slowly come closer to the ground. Deanna jumped off "WHALE ROCK" and began to swim to shore onto the beach. She ran past one of her beautiful sandcastles she had started earlier that day, past the ripe blueberries on the path and came upon the opening where the flying machine had already landed. As the dust cleared, there stood the Bug'z Travis, Taylor and Sam, arms opened wide. Deanna ran into the middle... Bug'z N' Hug'z. "What are you doing here?" she said with much excitement. Travis answered, "Well I thought we would drop in for a visit and "DROP" we did!!" "A visit!!" said Deanna Driftwood. "What of the Island?" she said. "The Island will be fine," said Travis. "It's just been too long, since we have done some TRAVLIN," all the Bug'z said at once. Deanna smiled, but could tell there was something more to their story, she was just so happy to see her cousin Travis and the others, she knew it could wait, but for how long. "Come!! You must be tired from your journey, my "Hut" is not far from here and I have a nice hammock for you Sam," she said smiling at Sam. "Sam has a small job to do for us first, he can meet us shortly and take a rest in that hammock that he so truly deserves," said Travis and Taylor agreed. Sam got right to his task and in no time the machine was fixed better than ever. Not only did he check that nut, he went over every nut on the flying machine, a second and third time. "What took you so long Sam?" asked Deanna, as Sam came to the screen door of her Hut.

"I stopped for some blueberries and lost track of time," said Sam as he winked at Travis. "How can you lose track of time?" said Taylor. They all laughed. After hours of catching up and telling stories of Travlin the world, Deanna finally asked Travis, "Why are you really here?" Travis began to tell her what had happened on the Island and how they had been captured, placed in jars, going to be put on exhibit for the whole world to see, the adventure on the ship, the escape from the trunks and everything. Then Sam spoke up, "In all of this that seemed bad, there was the "little one", and they all agreed." More of her kind should be like her, the one who set us free." "Deanna, our secret is out, that's why we are here and now we must warn the others," said Travis...

END OF CHAPTER TEN

CHAPTER ELEVEN

The Guardian's Club, our secret is safe

Guardian's oath certificate
I Sophie pledge to
do anything in my
power to protect,
assist and provide
care for DEANNA
who was placed
under my protection.
By doing so, I am now
a valued member of
the Travlin Bug'z.
Guardian's club.

Sophie : 8-1-01.

Our secret is safe.

Right then Deanna turned from green to red. "What is it Deanna?" said the Bug'z. "Are you O.K.?" Deanna stood there, still as the water perfect for skipping stones. Then she spoke. "You have to meet Sophie." "Who is Sophie?" said the Bug'z all at once, as they began buzzing about. "Sophie!! None of us know a Sophie, and we know all "THE TRAVLINBUG'Z." Deanna sat them down after the buzzing had stopped. "The "little one" you speak of is not the only one of her kind that is good." The Bug'z were silent as Deanna had begun to tell of her "little one", her own Guardian. "We made an oath. Sophie pledged to protect and keep my secret as secret as she could and help me on my journeys around the world. I think you should meet her, she knows all about you." Travis, Taylor and Sam could not believe what they were hearing. Deanna had made contact with a human, much like they had, long ago. "A "little one!!" said Sam. "Can we meet her," he said in his excited voice. Travis and Taylor were not so happy about what they were hearing. They had all been entrusted with the Island and their secret. Up until this point, they had done a great job for many, many, many years!! "You have befriended a human, "little one." How is this possible, were you captured and released by her, like we were?" said Travis. "No!!" said Deanna. "We are friends, she makes sure I am safe and watched over when I am here on the Island. I was with her this morning before you dropped in. We were building a sandcastle at our favorite beach." "A castle built from sand? Is that structurally safe? Why sand, that doesn't seem right on a beach, what of the waves, do you design a wall to stop the water? I have so many questions," said Taylor. Travis just sat there, then he spoke. "Are all the larger humans different than the "little ones"? said Travis. "What do you mean?" said Deanna. "Well, the "little ones" seem to be more helpful and happy. When they get larger do they change?" said Travis. "Well as Sophie tells me, some humans as they get larger lose their inner child and forget the little things that make them who they are. All the larger ones have a child inside them still, but some forget to let it out as often as they should she tells me. The others are just big "little ones" like Hugh and Mother, you told me about," said Deanna. "We must meet her!!" The Bug'z said all at once. "Sure!!" said Deanna. "Follow me, we can get fresh blueberries on the way."

END OF CHAPTER ELEVEN

CHAPTER TWELVE

Sophie's Surprise

A "little one"

82

As the four Bug'z came to the end of the dirt road heading to the beach, they could hear someone whistling. "That's her, that's Sophie!!" said Deanna. "Come on let's meet her. She is probably worried about me, she takes me with her wherever she goes. Sometimes I just hang on her backpack and enjoy the ride, Sophie!!" yelled Deanna as loud as she could, but there was no response. She just kept whistling and working alone. "She has her IPod on listening to music I bet." The three Bug'z just looked at one another, they had never heard of such a device. "May I take a closer look?" said Taylor. Deanna handed over her favorite possession in the world.

Suddenly, Sophie felt something brush against her legs, it was Sam's wings. As she looked down to check out what it was, she could not believe her eyes. Standing there were four TravlinBug'z. As she pulled off her headphones, she scooped up Deanna Driftwood, held her gently in the palm of her hand and said, "Where were you, I was worried sick, are you ok?" who are your friends... Dee?" Deanna began to explain, what had happened to Travis, Taylor and Sam. "Well not all of us are the way those two were back then. Your secret is safe with me, I took an oath. Deanna and I are the best of friends and I will do anything in my power to protect her. We even formed our own club,

The TravlinBug'z Guardians Club. What do you think of the title, cool..." said Sophie. The Bug'z stood there in the sand, by the castle - Sam in amazement, Taylor trying to figure out the structure and how it was only made out of sand, and Travis proud of how his little cousin had turned out. She had become the "BUG" he knew she could be when she left the Island so long ago. Being the youngest of the Bug'z she had a real sense of who she was and Travis was amazed at that and what had occurred between her and her Guardian. Maybe it was time to move on and warn the others, he felt that Deanna Driftwood was in good hands, safe and protected, most of all loved by her, "little one".

As they all gathered together, Taylor spoke up, "I think it is time for us to be TRAVLIN on, Deanna is in good hands Travis. Sam is fully rested and we have many others we have to warn. By the way, who is next?" asked Taylor. They climbed aboard the flying machine to start their next journey.

END OF CHAPTER TWELVE

Where to next,
the adventure continues

"Who is it?"

"Travis your compass please," said Taylor. "Sam, a new ticket from your pocket please." Both of the Bug'z handed over their items without haste. Taylor pulled out her watch and put it into the strange little box once again. Suddenly it began to vibrate and buzz, making horrible noises. Nothing came out of the other end this time. Puzzled Taylor studied it for a moment, as Sam, with help from Travis, harnessed up for a long flight. Taylor asked, "Deanna may I use your IPod please, I have an idea." "Sure!!" said Deanna, handing over her device. "What for?" she asked. "I have a suspicion as to why it's not working," said Taylor. There is a small hole in the side, I did not know what it was for when I constructed it, but now I have an idea what it is for. You see we all have something special we carry with us, maybe finding you first was meant to be, maybe this is the piece we need to find the next Bug." As Taylor plugged it into the strange little box, the compass began to move and her watch had began to spin backwards. Suddenly out of control, out of the other end, like before, came a colorful postcard with a picture on it. "Who is it?" they all said at once to Taylor. As she held it up, they all smiled. SANDI DOLA no words, just latitude and longitude of her whereabouts. The next to be

warned that their secret is "OUT."
In the case of Deanna, "OUT" was
a good thing safe in the hands of
her Guardian. "Is she with HANGER
ARMSTRONG?" Deanna asked. "WE"...
will have to wait and see. They usually
are "TRAVLIN" together... Sandi,
always looking to add to her collection,
and Hanger always searching for the
"PERFECT WAVE"... After some long
good-byes, more BUG'Z N' HUG'Z.
The Bug'z headed out from the Island
to their next destination, turning
southeast they began to wave goodbye
to Deanna and Sophie standing atop
Whale Rock. As Taylor calculated
their course, the three Bug'z took
their last glimpse of the two jumping

off the rock together splashing and playing. Taylor spoke up and said, "The main nut is tight, right boys!! The cotter pin is in and safe, we are going to be "TRAVLIN" for a while." Travis and Sam just looked at each other, then both at Taylor. She smiled, then reached into her pouch and pulled out one of her journals... and began writing...

END OF VOLUME TWO

Well... It could be worser!

Created in 2011, by author/artist J. Graham. The TravlinBug'z represent a positive model for today's youth, encouraging the idea of friendship and teamwork. Follow them along on their adventures at:

www.travlinbugz.com

Join in and protect your Bug'z from Victor Spoil'z.
Travis Passport, Taylor Timezone and Sam Stoaway travel the world warning the other Bug'z that their big secret has been discovered.

Use the TravlinBug'z as a means to link new and old friends together.